Ooh La La, Lottie!

KAREN WALLACE

Illustrated by

GARRY PARSONS

KINGFISHER

Dedicated to Gracie – K.W.
Pour Monsieur Cazier – G.P.

KINGFISHER

An imprint of Kingfisher Publications Plc
New Penderel House, 283-288 High Holborn
London WC1V 7HZ
www.kingfisherpub.com

First published by Kingfisher 2004
2 4 6 8 10 9 7 5 3 1

Text copyright © Karen Wallace 2004
Illustrations copyright © Garry Parsons 2004

A CIP catalogue record for this book
is available from the British Library.

ISBN 0 7534 0989 5

Printed in India
ITR/0604/AJT/GRS(GRS)/115SMA

Contents

Chapter One

Once there was a girl named Lottie
La Belle.

She lived with her mother and father
and a big white poodle called Patrick.

Lottie had thick black hair and
eyes as brown as chestnuts.

She always had her hair in pigtails.
She didn't care what clothes she wore.
Lottie was only interested
in one thing. She loved
playing with Patrick.

Every day, Lottie made Patrick a new
clip-on bow tie for his collar.

Every day, Patrick walked with Lottie
to school.

And when she did her homework,
he lay under her desk and kept her
feet warm.

When she went swimming, he watched
from the gallery.

Chapter Two

One evening, Lottie sat down to supper
in a bad mood.

Her trousers were ripped and the buttons
were missing from her shirt.

Her hair looked as if she had cut it with
a pair of garden shears.

"Ooh la la, Lottie!" cried Mrs La Belle.
"You look as messy as a dog's dinner."

Lottie glared at her
mother. She was so
annoyed she wanted
to do something
really naughty.

On the table was cauliflower in cream sauce with buttered peas, carrots and fresh green beans.

It was Lottie's favourite supper but now she didn't care.

"If I look as messy as a dog's dinner I won't eat a dinner a dog wouldn't eat."

Lottie pushed her plate away.

"Patrick hates vegetables. So do I."

Mr La Belle twitched his moustache.

"Will you eat dog food then?" he
asked sternly.

On the other side of the room was a plate
of cheese and biscuits.

A brilliant idea popped into Lottie's mind.

"Of course I won't eat dog food," said
Lottie. "I shall eat bread and cheese.
Patrick likes cheese," she added quickly.
Mrs La Belle rolled her eyes.

"Ooh la la, Lottie!" she cried.
"Whatever will you think of next?"
From that moment on Lottie La Belle
ate bread and cheese.

She ate bread and
cheese for breakfast.

She ate bread and
cheese for lunch.

She ate bread and
cheese for supper.

13

It was the same the next week and the week after that.

"Don't you get fed up with bread and cheese?" asked her friend Jeanette.

"No," said Lottie. "I like it."

She smiled and Jeanette noticed
something rather strange.

Lottie's front teeth had grown long
and sharp.

Her ears were strangely furry.

That night Lottie didn't sleep in her bed. She curled up inside a pile of leaves she had hidden in her cupboard.

Chapter Three

The next day Lottie had a piano lesson.
But when Lottie sat down on the
bench, the teacher's eyes popped out
of his head.
A tail was hanging from the hem
of Lottie's skirt!

In the afternoon Lottie painted a picture of herself. When the teacher saw it, she jumped onto a chair and screamed. It was a picture of a mouse!

Lottie's parents were called to the school immediately.

"I'm sorry to inform you that your daughter has turned into a mouse," said the headmaster.

"Ooh la la, Lottie!" cried Mrs La Belle. "Whatever shall we do?"

"Take her to the vet," said the headmaster.

"No child of mine will go to a vet," shouted Mr La Belle. "She might catch fleas in the waiting room! I shall take her to a doctor immediately."

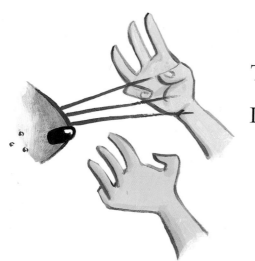

The doctor counted
Lottie's whiskers.

She shone a torch
in Lottie's
furry ears.

She measured the
length of Lottie's tail.

"She is definitely a mouse," the doctor said.

"Whatever shall we do?" cried Mrs La Belle.

"She must not eat any more cheese," said the doctor firmly.

"She must eat only vegetables."

"But I like being a mouse," said
Lottie La Belle.

And she scampered out of the room
before anyone could catch her.

Chapter Four

It didn't matter what kind of
vegetables Mrs La Belle cooked.
It didn't matter whether they were
raw, fried, steamed or roasted.
Lottie would not eat them.
After a while, Mrs La Belle gave up.

She swept the leaves from her daughter's cupboard instead of making her bed. She even cut holes in Lottie's trousers so her tail would be more comfortable.

Mr La Belle gave up, too.

He didn't read Lottie fairy stories any more.

She didn't like them because the princes
and princesses weren't mice.

So Mr La Belle read her mouse
adventures and changed the endings
so the mice always won.

As for Patrick, he was very sad because Lottie didn't play with him any more. She was too busy making nests under the sofa or looking for crumbs on the floor.

Poor Patrick! Most days he lay outside the back door.

Chapter Five

One day, Lottie's friend Jeanette
came to visit.

"Why don't you come to school any
more?" she asked.

Lottie crawled out from behind
the sofa.

"Mice don't go to school," she said,
as she nibbled a piece of hard cheese.

"Mice don't like lessons."

Jeanette stared at her feet.

"Do mice like swimming?" she asked
at last.

Lottie cocked her head to one side and
pulled thoughtfully at a whisker.

"I'm not sure."

Mrs La Belle looked up from where she was cutting out mouse-shaped biscuits.

"Ooh la la, Lottie!" she cried. "Of course mice like swimming!"

Patrick lifted
Lottie's swimming
bag from its hook
in the back hall
and stood in the
kitchen wagging his tail.
"Very well," said Lottie. "I shall go."
So Lottie and Jeanette went to the
swimming pool and Patrick
sat in the gallery.
A moment later,
Jeanette jumped
into the
pool.

Lottie stood by the side. She looked at the water and suddenly she felt very afraid. Her mother wasn't right at all!

"Lottie!" cried Jeanette.

"What's wrong?"

"Mice do NOT like swimming!"
shouted Lottie.
And without another word, she
disappeared.

Chapter Six

One day, Lottie was sitting in the garden chewing an apple pip.

An apple pip was quite big for Lottie, because as time passed she had become smaller and smaller.

Now she was more like a mouse than ever.

Lottie swallowed the apple pip and
bit into another.

She didn't take much notice when the
cat from next door sat down beside her.

Then he moved closer and she smelled
his hot, hungry, catty breath.

Suddenly, she knew she was in danger!
"Help! Help!" shouted Lottie. "The cat
wants to eat me!"
But Mrs La Belle didn't hear because
Lottie's shout was only as loud as a
mouse's squeak.

Lottie jumped up and ran across the grass.

The cat ran after her.

"Help! Help!" she cried again.

This time Patrick pricked up his ears.

Quick as a flash he jumped

onto the grass.

Then he chased the cat away just as it
was about to gobble Lottie up!

Lottie lay on the ground and howled.
Patrick howled, too.
He hated to see
Lottie unhappy.

Mrs La Belle ran into the garden.

"I don't want to be a mouse any more," sobbed Lottie. "I want to be a little girl again."

Mrs La Belle kissed Lottie's furry pink ears.

"Then you must do what the doctor told you," she said.

Chapter Seven

The doctor was right.

After a week of eating her vegetables,

Lottie was almost a little girl again.

One day, when she was completely
better, Lottie came down to supper.
On the table was cauliflower in a cream
sauce with buttered peas, carrots and
fresh green beans.
"Yum! Vegetables!" cried Lottie.

"I love vegetables!"

And she helped herself to lots of

everything.

Mr La Belle twitched his moustache.

"What about Patrick?" he asked,

slowly. "You said he hated vegetables."

"Patrick has changed his mind!" said
Lottie La Belle with a grin. She put
down her knife and fork and whistled.

Patrick trotted into the room with a
huge carrot in his mouth.

Lottie had cut it in the shape of a bone!

Mr La Belle burst out laughing.

"Ooh la la, Lottie!" cried Mrs La Belle.

"Whatever will you think of next?"

About the Author and Illustrator

Karen Wallace is an award-winning writer and has published over 90 books for children.

"Ooh La La, Lottie! was based on a little girl I met in France when my son was on an exchange visit," says Karen. "I love writing funny books because I get to laugh at my own jokes."

Garry Parsons is an illustrator of children's books, magazines and advertisements. He likes to draw and paint all day. Garry says "Like Lottie, I love eating lots of bread and cheese. I wonder what animal she would have turned into if she had eaten a lot of something else, like bananas or sardines!"

Tips for Beginner Readers

1. Think about the cover and the title of the book. What do you think it will be about? While you are reading, think about what might happen next and why.

2. As you read, ask yourself if what you're reading makes sense. If it doesn't, try rereading or look at the pictures for clues.

3. If there is a word that you do not know, look carefully at the letters, sounds and word parts that you do know. Blend the sounds to read the word. Is this a word you know? Does it make sense in the sentence?

4. Think about the characters, where the story takes place, and the problems the characters in the story faced. What are the important ideas in the beginning, middle and end of the story?

5. Ask yourself questions like:
Did you like the story?
Why or why not?
How did the author make it fun to read?
How well did you understand it?

Maybe you can understand the story better if you read it again!